STEP-BY-STEP EXPERIMENTS WITH SOUND

By Gina Hagler

Illustrated by Bob Ostrom

The Child's World®

Published by The Child's World®
1980 Lookout Drive • Mankato, MN 56003-1705
800-599-READ • www.childsworld.com

ACKNOWLEDGMENTS
The Child's World®: Mary Berendes, Publishing Director
The Design Lab: Design and production
Red Line Editorial: Editorial direction
Consultant: Dr. Peter Barnes, Assistant Scientist, Astronomy Dept.,
University of Florida

ISBN 9781609735937
LCCN 2011940149

Design elements: Pilar Echeverria/Dreamstime, Robisklp/Dreamstime,
Sarit Saliman/Dreamstime, Jeffrey Van Daele/Dreamstime

Printed in the United States of America
Mankato, MN
May 2013
PA02182

BE SAFE!

The experiments in this book are meant for kids to do themselves. Sometimes an adult's help is needed though. Look in the supply list for each experiment. It will list if an adult is needed. Also, some supplies will need to be bought by an adult.

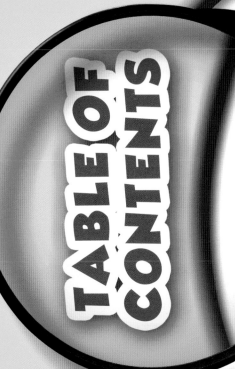

TABLE OF CONTENTS

The sounds that birds and dogs make are very different.

CHAPTER ONE

Study Sound!

Have you heard a bird's chirp or a dog's growl? Do you wonder why some noises sound high while others are low? Sound is everywhere. We speak using sound. Different sounds tell us different information. Sounds let us know if something is close or far. Other sounds let us know if there is danger. People and animals use sound every day.

How is sound heard? Sound is energy that moves in **sound waves**. These sound waves are all around us. They move through the air, water, and objects. Sound waves strike our **eardrums**. Our brain turns vibrations into the sounds we hear. How can you learn more about sound?

CHAPTER TWO

Seven Science Steps

Doing a science experiment is a fun way to discover new facts! An experiment follows steps to find answers to science questions. This book has experiments to help you learn about sound. You will follow the same seven steps in each experiment:

Seven Steps

1. **Research**: Figure out the facts before you get started.

2. **Question**: What do you want to learn?

3. **Guess**: Make a prediction. What do you think will happen in the experiment?

4. **Gather**: Find the supplies you need for your experiment.

5. **Experiment**: Follow the directions.

6. **Review**: Look at the results of the experiment.

7. **Conclusion**: The experiment is done. Now it is time to reach a conclusion. Was your prediction right?

Are you ready to become a scientist? Let's experiment to learn about sound!

Ocean water and sound both travel in waves.

CHAPTER THREE

What Is a Wave?

Have you seen waves in the ocean? The waves move from the deep water to the beach. Sound waves also move from one point to another. Try this experiment to see how waves move.

Research the Facts

Here are a few. What else do you know?

- A **frequency** is the number of vibrations a sound makes each second.
- Waves have a **crest** and a **trough**. The crest is the high point of a wave. The trough is the low point of the wave.
- A **wavelength** is the distance between two crests of a wave.

Ask Questions

- What happens as a wave moves away from the place where it starts?
- How does a wave look when it moves fast or slow?

Make a Prediction

Here are two examples:

- A fast wave has a short wavelength.
- A fast wave has a long wavelength.

- A friend
- A jump rope
- Pencil or pen
- Paper

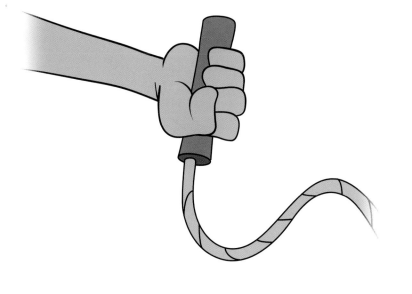

Time to Experiment!

1. Hold one end of the jump rope. Ask a friend to hold the other end.

2. Slowly move your arm up and down to make the jump rope move. Ask your friend to stay still.

3. Look at how the jump rope moves. Stop and record what you see.

4. Now, move your arm quickly. Record how the jump rope moves.

5. Stay still. Ask your friend to move the jump rope up and down slowly.

6. Look at how the jump rope moves. Stop and record what you see.

7. Ask your friend to move his or her arm up and down quickly. Record how the jump rope moves now.

Review the Results

Did you notice how the rope moved? It wiggled. Those wiggles are waves. Each wave moved up and down. The energy moved along the rope, making waves as it moved. The waves were short when the jump rope moved quickly. The waves were long when the jump rope moved slowly.

What Is Your Conclusion?

Waves formed when you moved one end of the jump rope up and down. Your hand's energy moved to the other end of the jump rope. Sound moves in waves like these. Sound starts at one point and moves to another point. Sound moves in a wavelength. The wavelengths can be short or long.

Sound waves bounce against our eardrums.

14

CHAPTER FOUR

Can You Hear Me Now?

Sound waves move through the air. See if sound waves can also move along a string.

Research the Facts

Here are a few. What other facts can you find?

- Our eardrums vibrate when sound waves hit them.
- Sound waves can lose energy as they move.

Ask Questions

- Can sound waves travel over a piece of string?
- Can you hear sound that moves along an object?

Make a Prediction

Here are two examples.

- Sound waves can move along a string.
- Sound waves cannot move along a string.

Gather Your Supplies!

- Adult help
- 2 thick cardboard cups (like the ones found in coffee shops)
- A nail
- 3 feet (1 m) of string
- A friend
- Pencil or pen
- Paper

Time to Experiment!

1. Ask an adult to do this step. Push the nail through the middle of the bottom of each cup.

2. Put the string through one of the holes. Tie a knot to keep it from pulling through. The knot should be inside the cup.

3. Do the same thing with the other cup. The other end of the string will be in this cup.

4. Hold one cup in your hand. Ask your friend to hold the other cup. Stand far apart. Make sure the string is tight and straight.

5. Put the cup over your ear.

6. Ask your friend to say something into his or her cup.

7. Record what happens.

8. Now stand closer together. Let the string sag.

9. Listen into the cup while your friend speaks into his or her cup. Record what happens.

Review the Results

Could you hear what your friend said? Did it matter if the rope was tight or loose? You could hear what your friend said when the string was tight. You could not hear what your friend said when the string was loose.

What Is Your Conclusion?

The string needs to be tight for sound waves to move along it. The vibrations move without losing a lot of energy on a tight string. On a loose string, vibrations are lost into the air. The vibrations from the string made the bottom of the cup vibrate. That made the air in the cup vibrate. That made your eardrum vibrate. That is how you heard the sound.

In older telephones, wires do the same thing that string does in this experiment. Sound waves become an electric signal. This signal travels over wires. This brings sound to another telephone.

Sound can move as an electric signal.

Can you hear sound through a table?

CHAPTER FIVE

Knock Three Times

You can hear sound waves in the air. Try this experiment to see if you can hear sound waves in solids, too.

Research the Facts

Here are a few. What else do you know?

- Sound waves can move through solids.
- A solid object is something that has a shape that does not change. It does not take on the shape of a container, like liquids or gases do.

Ask Questions

- Is a sound louder when it travels through the air or an object?
- Does your ear need to touch an object to hear a sound in the object?

Gather Your Supplies!

- A friend
- A long wood table
- Pencil or pen
- Paper

Make a Prediction

Here are two examples:

- Sound is louder in an object.
- Sound is louder in the air.

Time to Experiment!

1. Ask your friend to stand at one end of the table. You should stand at the other end.

2. Knock three times on the table.

3. Have your friend record what she or he heard. Was it loud? Rate the sound from zero to ten. Zero is very quiet. Ten is very loud.

4. Ask your friend to put his or her ear on the table.

5. Knock three times on the table.

6. Ask your friend to rate the sound again. Was it loud or quiet? Write it down in your notes.

7. Now repeat steps 1 to 6. This time listen while your friend knocks. Record how it sounds in your notes.

Review the Results

What did you hear? You could hear the knocking in the air. You could also hear it when your ear was on the table. The knocking was louder when your ear was on the table.

What Is Your Conclusion?

Sound travels better through a solid, such as the table. It does not travel as well through a gas, such as air. All of the sound waves move through the table. In the air, some sound waves can move in different directions. The vibrations spread out and lose a lot of energy. That makes the sound quieter. In the table, the vibrations move quickly from one point to another point. The sound waves move in one direction. This makes the sound louder when your ear touches the table.

Sound waves travel fastest through solids. They are slower in liquids. And they are slowest in gases.

CHAPTER SIX

Making Waves

Sound waves travel through liquid. And sound waves can come from two different points. Try this experiment to see what happens if waves meet.

Research the Facts

Here are a few. What other facts do you know?

- Waves move through water. They start at one point and move to another point.
- Sound comes from many directions.

Waves move out from a point in the water.

Ask Questions

- Do sound waves meet?

- What happens if sound waves meet?

Make a Prediction

Here are two examples:

- Sound waves go right past each other without stopping.

- Sound waves get in each other's way and slow down or stop.

Gather Your Supplies!

- Water
- A baking dish with sides
- Marbles
- Pencil or pen
- Paper

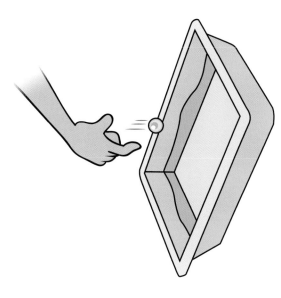

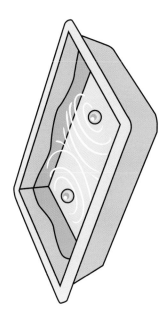

Time to Experiment!

1. Fill the baking dish half full with water.

2. Drop a marble into the water.

3. Watch what happens. Write down what you see.

4. Take the marble out. Wait for the water to be still again.

5. Drop two marbles in the water at the same time. Put them in different spots in the dish.

6. Watch the two sets of waves. Do they meet? What happens? Record what you see.

Review the Results

Did the marbles make waves? Did the two waves meet? When one marble hit the water, waves spread out in a circle from it. When two marbles were dropped in, two sets of waves were made. The waves met and made a new wave.

What Is Your Conclusion?

Two sound waves can meet and make a new sound wave. Like the waves in the water, two sounds can meet in the air. They make a new sound.

Have you seen and heard a band play? Sounds from the different instruments combine. A new sound is made. This is the band's song!

You are a scientist now. What fun sound facts did you learn? You found out that sound moves in waves. You learned that sound can be heard through solids. You can learn even more about sound. Study it. Experiment with it. Then share what you learn about sound.

Glossary

conclusion (kuhn-KLOO-shuhn): A conclusion is what you learn from doing an experiment. Her conclusion is that sound can move through a table.

crest (KREST): A crest is the top of something, such as a wave. A sound wave has a crest.

eardrums (IHR-druhmz): Eardrums are the parts of ears that vibrate when sound waves hit them. Your eardrums vibrate when you hear sounds.

frequency (FREE-kwuhn-see): A frequency is the number of vibrations each second in a sound wave. A sound with a high frequency has short waves.

prediction (pri-DIKT-shun): A prediction is what you think will happen in the future. His prediction was right that sound is loud in a solid.

signal (SIG-nuhl): A signal is a pulse of energy or electricity used in telephones, radio, and television. Sound moves as a signal in older telephones.

sound waves (SOUND WAYVZ): Sound waves are series of vibrations in the air, a solid, or a liquid that can be heard. Sound waves move from one point to another.

trough (TRAWF): A trough is the low point of a wave. A sound wave has a trough.

vibrate (VYE-brate): To vibrate is to move back and forth quickly. Sound waves make a person's eardrums vibrate.

wavelength (WAYV-length): A wavelength is the distance between one crest and the next in a sound wave. Sound waves can have a short or long wavelength.

Books

Brasch, Nicolas. *Why Does Sound Travel? All About Sound.* New York: PowerKids Press, 2010.

Hall, Pamela. *Listen! Learn About Sound.* Mankato, MN: The Child's World, 2011.

Trumbauer, Lisa. *All About Sound.* New York: Children's Press, 2004.

Woodford, Chris. *Experiments with Sound and Hearing.* New York: Gareth Stevens, 2010.

Index

ABOUT THE AUTHOR:

Gina Hagler is a freelance writer and educator covering science, technology, nature, and the environment for children and adults. She lives in the Maryland suburbs with her husband, three terrific kids, and a goofy dog named Brownie.